Emma Styles

Australian poems

Emma Styles

Australian poems

ISBN/EAN: 9783337241940

Printed in Europe, USA, Canada, Australia, Japan

Cover: Foto ©Andreas Hilbeck / pixelio.de

More available books at **www.hansebooks.com**

AUSTRALIAN POEMS

BY

EMMA STYLES,

AUTHOR OF "A HELPING HAND" AND "SCRAPS FROM MY
JOURNAL."

Adelaide :
W. K. Thomas & Co., Grenfell Street, Adelaide.
1883.

DEDICATED

TO

THE RIGHT REV.

THE

LORD BISHOP OF ADELAIDE

BY

PERMISSION.

PREFACE.

Having frequently filled up my leisure moments by
scribbling, without the slightest intention of presenting
my pieces to the public eye, acquaintances have done me
the honour on several occasions of requesting copies of
them, while others have advised their publication ; by
following this advice an opportunity is given of benefiting
a noble institution in the Colony, the "Home for In-
curables," to which purpose the profits arising from the
"Australian Poems" will be devoted.

Some years since on having a small collection printed
in aid of St. Augustine's Church, Unley, so much success
attended that undertaking that I am encouraged to help
forward another worthy object.

The Lord Bishop has kindly permitted me to dedicate
the book to him, and I trust that its publication will be
attended with success.

E. S.

Amersham Villa,
    Unley, South Australia,
        October, 1883.

An honour'd Institution this ; a Home
Where no creed separates, where all may come- -
Victims of an incurable disease—
For medical advice their pain to ease.
Now to the memory of Dr. Gosse we'd build
A wing, much needed.   Every ward is filled.
His name and fame are dear to all who knew
The skill'd physician, friend, adviser true ;
Not one within this Home but long will mourn
Him, their kind benefactor, from them gone ;
Each moisten'd eye bespeaks a love sincere
For Lim whose presence brought such comfort here ;
All miss the kindly converse, tender smile,
Which ofttimes did their weariness beguile ;
No suffering one, but lov'd his step to hear,
And suffered less the while he linger'd near.

ERRATA.

Page 11, in verse 2, at end of first line insert the word " morn."

Page 16, in first and third lines, read " have" for " has."

Page 68, in first line of last verse but one, read " busy" for " bitter."

Page 112, read " To walk over green grass, so soft to the tread," in place of the third line.

INDEX.

	PAGE
IMPROMPTU	1
FRIENDSHIP	4
NOT LOST ...	5
CABIN MUSINGS IN ROUGH WEATHER	7
THE YOUNG WIDOW	8
THE PET OF THE SHIP	11
I CANNOT THINK OF THEE	13
WATCHING ...	14
FOUND ON THE BEACH	17
THE LIGHT OF THE HOME ...	19
MARRIAGE LINES	21
GO FORTH, MY CHILD	22
CAPE TOWN, SOUTH AFRICA	25
HOW SWEET IT IS ...	27
ONLY A PICTURE	29
TO A BOY ON THE STEP OF AN OMNIBUS	31
A SEASIDE SKETCH	33
IN MEMORIAM, DR. BAYER ...	38
THE SECOND GRIEF	40
WINTER'S COMING IN ENGLAND	42
ON A FRIEND'S ENGAGEMENT	43
MARRIAGE LINES	44
GOING HOME	45
DEDICATED TO ——— AT THEIR JUBILEE WEDDING	48

INDEX.

	PAGE
HOMEWARD BOUND	50
INTEMPERANCE	52
AN INVALID'S DEATH	54
WELCOME TO AN INFANT	56
THE YOUNG PASTOR'S WIFE	57
AT REST FOR EVER	60
TO ——— ON LEAVING TASMANIA	63
BUCKS, ENGLAND	65
AN ENGLISH VILLAGE CHURCHYARD SCENE	67
DEATH'S NARRATION	69
THE MEMORY OF THE PAST	72
ON THE BIRTH OF THE FIRSTBORN	74
HAPPY IS HE	76
IN MEMORIAM	77
OUR HOLIDAY RIDE	79
SABBATH AT SEA	88
EVENING PRAYER AT SEA	89
PARTINGS	91
VANISHED HOPES	93
DEDICATION OF AN INFANT	94
NEVER NURSE A SORROW	96
THE WORLD IS WHAT WE MAKE IT	98
LITTLE CHILD AT PRAYER	101
DREAMING	103
THE WRECK OF THE GOTHENBURG	104
CHRISTMAS	110
IN THE COUNTRY	112
SLEEPING	113
THE WANDERER'S FAREWELL	114
TO MY PEN	116

IMPROMPTU.

Land of my birth, my native land, I love thy name to
    hear,
For on thy far-off peaceful shore dwell all of kindred dear.
A tiny child they brought me far away across the sea,
So young without a sigh or pang I left both them and
    thee.
Have dwelt a child, a woman grown, upon this foreign
    shore—
Then chide me not—England I love, but fair Australia
    more.

The greatness of that empire vast with wonder doth
    inspire
Her statesmen ; all her mighty men of learning I admire,
And fain would feast mine eyes on all the splendour of
    her state,
Her spacious halls filled with rich works of art and science
    great ;
Each cherished spot, each ruin old would joy to wander
    o'er—
Yet chide me not—England I love, but fair Australia
    more.

Here mountain range and valley resound with wild birds'
  song ;
Here dwells a happy people—brave, independent, strong.
Of great nations' pomps and vanities and poverty I've
  read,
Here in this land of plenty no creature need want bread.
Disease, and want, and misery tread not our happy shore—
Then chide me not—England I love, but fair Australia
  more.

How many by consumption warn'd set sail for this far
  shore :
Where health and strength return again when life seem'd
  all but o'er ;
Where bright blue skies above them are in cloudless
  beauty seen,
Where nature smiles on hill and plain, all deck'd in
  glorious sheen ;
At ripe old age they gently fall asleep upon our shore—
Then chide me not—England I love, but fair Australia
  more.

In the land of my adoption where peace and plenty dwell,
Heaven sheds her richest blessings and prospers all things
  well,
We reap a bounteous harvest from fertile vale and plain,
And send to starving thousands the precious golden grain.
Here I have passed my childhood's days—would rest
  when life is o'er—
Then chide me not—England I love, but dear Australia
  more.

Yet while to me Australia is the dearest spot on earth,
My heart oft longs to see again the old land of my birth,
The land where my forefathers dwelt, where dear ones yet
    remain
To welcome me, whose faces I shall joy to see again.
But should I pine for this fair land and wish my sojourn
    o'er,
Oh! chide me not—England I love, but dear Australia
    more.

Farewell Australia—loving friends I bid farewell to thee
What happy memories will be mine when far across the
    sea.
No scenes of wonder, friendships new, will banish from
    my mind,
The beauties of this sunny clime and those I leave behind.
If heaven permit, what joy again to stand upon thy
    shore—
My native land—England I love, but fair Australia more.

FRIENDSHIP.

Friendship, kind hallow'd fellowship of heart,
Thou dost to mortals purest joys impart ;
Friends, they who share with us the joys of life,
Who aid us in our battlings with strife,
Who seek us when by grief our hearts are bow'd,
And point out silver lining in dark cloud,
Support us when death some dear tie has riv'n,
Direct our trembling gaze from earth to heaven ;
For whom like blessèd privilege we claim,
In joy and sorrow ours to do the same,
Whose love like clear and constant burning light
Illumes our way, and ever guides aright ;
Sheds hallow'd influence within our home —
Fond memories clinging wheresoe'er we roam ;
When seas divide, we sojourn in strange lands,
They seem to beckon us with gentle hands ;
When we regain the dear familiar shore,
Their welcome is as hearty as of yore.
Friendship, the richest gift kind heaven doth give,
Without thee what were life ? Who'd wish to live ?
Begun on earth, fulfilled beyond the sky,
Death cannot sever friendship's blessèd tie.

NOT LOST.

No, we have not lost our darling,
   He has only gone away,
For he heard the angels calling,
   And he could no longer stay.

No, we have not lost our Eddie,
   Though we miss him everywhere,
Though we seem to wait his coming,
   Gazing on his empty chair.

Jesus, ever-tender Shepherd,
   Marked our little tired sheep ;
In His arms He gently bore him,
   There our Eddie fell asleep.

Little life-work to him given ;
   All accomplished—he is gone ;
Like a dream his brief existence ;
   Floweret culled at early morn.

Ere life's battle-cry had sounded,
   Death has loosed the silver cord ;
In the strife he might have fallen,
   Now dear Eddie's safe with God.

Oft amid life's weary warfare,
   When we shed affliction's tear,
We shall feel our darling Eddie
   Is far better there than here.

When the call to us is given,
  And we cling to those we love,
Earth's ties will be easier riven
  When we think of those above.

No, we have not lost our Eddie—
  Happy spirit, angel bright,
Fairer than we e'er beheld him,
  Where there's neither sin nor night.

No, we have not lost our darling,
  For the blessèd never die,
And dear ones on earth we cherished
  Live immortal in the sky.

CABIN MUSINGS IN ROUGH WEATHER.

[MIDNIGHT ON A STEAMER; SOUNDS OF DISTRESS.]

Obnoxious place, where fancy never leads,
Save when necessity hath urgent needs ;
When sickness such as landsmen never know
Bids us poor mortals hurry to and fro.
My pen lacks power of language to express
All here endured of pain and helplessness.
O horrid sanctum ! thy polluted air
Sickens my very soul—but pen forbear,
Or thou wilt coward make me ; it were vain,
While yet afloat, doomed to return again,
Oh ! for the morn to break, that I awhile
Might on the deck, and quit these regions vile.
I care not for the gale—the gale may blow—
In my rug on deck no *mal-de-mer* I know ;
With scorn I'll leave thee ; would that nevermore
Unwilling steps should near thy dreaded door ;
Nature's last bidding done, what joy to fly
From thee ; of thee may all remembrance die.

THE YOUNG WIDOW.

Why were they parted?   Man and wife :
They were not old, nor tired of life,
Nor weary of its care and strife.

Why were they separated?   None may know,
Save He alone who dealt the cruel blow,
And laid the fondest, best of husbands low.

Naught in their wedded lives amiss,
A happy dream of hallowed bliss,
But passed away so soon as this.

Each day bore testimony how
Well they performed their marriage vow ;
And yet they are divided now.

Sweet children unto them were given :
And still it was the will of heaven
Home's dearest ties should thus be riven.

It does seem strange death did not spare
Such a devoted, loving pair ;
Part—some less happy than they were.

The fond wife watched his bed of pain,
Tended him lovingly in vain,
For he was not to rise again.

"Behold, I come," the Spirit saith;
She bent to catch his last faint breath—
How could she yield him up to death?

"Oh! leave him with us, Lord," she cried,
And would have kept him at her side;
But prayers and wishes were denied.

In bitter grief and anguish sore,
She watched the final struggle o'er:
The bright sun set to rise no more.

She stood alone—a widow lone;
The greatest grief her heart had known;
Life's darkest shadow o'er her thrown.

Alone in this great world of sin;
To keep those young hearts pure within,
Without his aid their way to win.

We know how hard to realize,
When one we love so dearly dies,
And but cold clay before our eyes.

We cannot stay the mourners' tears,
Or calm the gloomy, anxious fears,
Or fill the void in coming years.

His little ones will question why
God let their dear, kind father die,
And took him from them to the sky?

We ask ourselves oft and again
Why he was taken, but in vain ;
God's ways man never can make plain.

The fatherless and widow's Friend
Will help and comfort to them send,
Will be their Guide unto the end.

And in His own good time restore
Their dear one when life's day is o'er,
When separation is no more.

THE PET OF THE SHIP.

Beautiful babe, with bright sparkling blue e'e,
No wonder thy parents so dote upon thee:
Little brow fair as the beautiful snow ;
Baby cheeks tinted with health's pretty glow
Smiles always playing on each tiny lip—
Wee thing of beauty, the Pet of the Ship.

Welcom'd with smiles by each one every
Miss'd when to snug little cot thou art borne
Till, like the warbling of sweet early bird,
Infantile prattle at day's dawn is heard ;
At first streak of light ere our last sleep we've had,
Thy clear, merry voice is repeating "Dad ! dad!"
When quickly proud nurse hurries off with a skip,
Away to the deck with the Pet of the Ship.

When the breezes of ocean to stiff gales do blow,
With her precious wee charge Phemie walks to and fro,
Though the good ship is rolling she fears not a fall,
And bright eyes peep at her from out of warm shawl ;
But pressing a kiss on the bluey cold lip,
She holds closer to her, the Pet of the Ship.

Little hands stretch'd out for Pa's chain of gold,
Grasping it tightly, determined to hold ;
Bright blue eyes dancing with babyish glee
When it is loosen'd and held up for thee.

Loving to sit upon Ma's lap so much,
To play with her hair, her jewels to touch ;
Little plump fists in work-basket to dip
Where is some pretty work for the Pet of the Ship.

Play'd with and talk'd to by young and by old,
Toss'd in the air by the jolly tars bold ;
No one e'er passes by nurse but must stay
Just a moment or two with dear baby to play,
When a caper of joy, with a smile on her lip,
They get in return from the Pet of the Ship.

Young parents so proud of their sweet first-born one,
Much thou'lt be miss'd when our voyage is done,
Daily dear babe we've grown fonder of thee !
Taken some part in thy innocent glee,
A plaything for all, thou'st enliven'd our trip,
And dear to our hearts is the Pet of the Ship.

We shall bid thee adieu when we reach England's shore,
And, perchance, pretty child, we shall see thee no more ;
Kind wishes from all will be thine when we part,
Though strangers, thy pretty ways won every heart.
Years hence, o'er the past memory fondly will skip,
And picture, dear baby, the Pet of the Ship.

Sweet child, may thy voyage o'er life's ocean be fair,
Though the storm-clouds of life gather everywhere ;
We fear not thy future, but trust One above—
We know thou'lt be reared in His fear and His love.
O'er the billows that roll may thy bark lightly skip—
May we meet in that haven, the Pet of the Ship !

I CANNOT THINK OF THEE.

I cannot think of thee, but what belovèd one,
My heart will wildly throb and blinding tears will come,
With the thought of joys which were, but will never be
again,
For thy friendship is denied me and brightest hopes are
vain.

I cannot hear the songs unmov'd that once I loved so
much,
To hear another sing them, how I miss thy voice and
touch ;
The sweet words are unalter'd, I listen, but somehow,
So touching is the melody, I cannot bear it now.

I cannot hear another sing those songs—but when alone,
With none to see my glistening eyes or mark my faltering
tone,
I strike the chords so gently and methinks I sing to thee,
As thou in happy days gone by hast often sang for me.

I cannot see thy picture without a thrill of pain,
It is so sad to turn away, so sweet to look again ;
A painful fascination seems about it like a spell,
A feeling we are parted—but have not said farewell.

I cannot hear thy name, but as it falls upon mine ear,
I feel I cannot realize thou art no longer here ;
Only when standing by thy grave I know that all is o'er,
And leave it trusting we shall meet where parting is no
more.

.

WATCHING.

Watching in the sick room
  With tender, patient care,
Woman, oh, how blessèd
  Is thy mission there!
Waiting on the sufferer
  As fond mother would ;
Or a gentle sister
  If they only could.
  .

Watching in the sick room,
  Where the lone one lies ;
Where, away from friends and home,
  Death will close his eyes.
Watcher, constant ever,
  Weary night and day ;
Ministering so tenderly
  To his wants alway.

Watching in the sick room,
  By the lone one sick ;
While thy heart is aching sore,
  While thy tears fall thick.
Bending o'er the sufferer
  Through the long, long night,
Looking oh, so anxiously,
  For the coming light.

Watching in the sick room,
  Where the daylight's dim ;
Where all friends and joys of life
  Are denied to him.
Telling of a Father's love,
  Of a Saviour near ;
Breathing words of comfort
  Softly in his ear.

Watching in the sick room,
  Leaving not for rest ;
All regardless quite of self—
  Woman, thou art blest.
God Almighty seeth thee,
  And thy work of love ;
Angels smile approvingly
  From their home above.

Watching in the sick room,
  By the lonely one ;
Angels watching o'er him, too,
  Till life's sands are run.
Long to shout triumphantly,
  Wait the soul's release ;
Eager now to welcome him
  To their home of peace.

Watching in the sick room,
  Soon thy watching o'er ;
Soon the sufferer's eyes will close
  Here for ever more.

Soon wjll they has looked their last
   On this world and thee ;
Soon the weary soul has past
   To Immortality.

Watching in the sick room :
   Sister do not weep,
Give he whom thou lov'st up
   To thy God to keep ;
Thou can'st do no more for him,
   Leave to God the rest ;
He it is who calleth him,
   And He knoweth best.

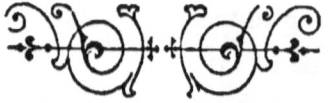

FOUND ON THE BEACH.

Beautiful woman, so lovely, so fair,
Salt spray gemming thy beautiful hair ;
Sea-weed encircling thy youthful brow,
'Never in life more lovely than now.
The slumber of death, thy last repose,
Where thou art sleeping nobody knows.
Near to thy side has the cruel wave thrown
Sweet little infant—is it thine own?
No simple ring on thy finger I see ;
Girlish and graceful thy form—can it be?
Art thou a mother, hast thou known care ?
Ah ! beautiful one, was thy beauty a snare?
Wert thou from happy home, basely beguil'd
Have parents sought sorrowing their erring child ?
O God ! if man has done this innocent wrong,
Thy vengeance will follow the guilty, the strong.
Was it unholy love, none other to blame,
Too heavy thy burden of sin, grief, and shame ;
In moment of frenzy, of suffering extreme,
Wert thou tempted to plunge in the dark, cold stream?
When night spread kind curtain of darkness to fly
Away from the living—determined to die ;
Seen only by One, ere bright morning's dawn,
Far out on the deep, babe and parent had gone,
He made thee so fair—O merciful God !
Is there pardon for those who loose life's silver cord?

Carried afar on the blue billows' crest,
Pressing the little one close to thy breast ;
Gentle waves bore thee again to the land,
Lifted thee tenderly up on the sand ;
Where the huge boulders near to thy head,
Tombstone shall be of the beautiful dead,
Carved to the memory of mother and child,
Washed by the breakers, when storm rages wild.
Heap up the sand for a grave hallowed mound,
Murmuring waves sing sad dirges around.

THE LIGHT OF THE HOME.

Picture such a child as you never saw before.
A beautiful child—age between three and four,
With head of luxuriant rich brown hair,
Large dark eyes, a bewitching pair,
Full of merriment, wonder, and glee ;
Gaze into their depths, they'll ever haunt thee,
Where'er she resides I truthfully tell,
She's acknowledged by all the miniature belle.

Dimple on cheek and dimple on chin,
Lips parting in smiles showing wee pearls within,
Voice clear as a bell, rich, dulcet, and sweet,
Like tripping of fairies the sound of her feet,
Blithesome and merry, tender and mild,
Truly indeed she's a loveable child.

Beseeching mamma for just one little ride
On the trycicle small, her dear brother's pride,
Seating herself, starting off all alone,
Along the verandah at speed of her own,
Guiding and gliding and wheeling about
With a dexterous grace, now in and now out ;
It's all very well and a rare treat the ride,
But the wee maiden blushes to know she's astride.

Her pet kitten, Queeny, must not be forgot,
It shares most of her pleasures, oft sleeps in her cot

With one plump arm around it, till governess goes
And steals it away during Ollee's repose ;
A sleek silky kitten, its mistress takes care
It has each meal of milk, enough and to spare.

Sweet innocent child, such rare graces showing,
May they as she grows be continually growing,
Tenderly nurtur'd—such now is she ;
What in the future ? what will she be ?
Whatever her lot, where'er she may roam
May she be the " blessing of somebody's home."

MARRIAGE LINES.

The sun is shining brightly for the bride elect, dear one,
It is thy bridal morn this day thy new life is begun,
So happy has thy girlhood been I ask thou mayest share
Much of the joy of wedded life and little of its care.

A wife ! Thy consort's little child thou'rt willing now to
    tend,
A great responsibility, thy work of love, dear friend,
A holy and a happy charge this day to thee is given,
To be a mother to that child to guide its steps to heaven.

Unweariedly and tenderly thou wilt perform that part,
Thy pure unselfish love will quickly win its infant heart.
God grant thee strength in wisdom's way his tiny feet to
    guide,
Should sickness lay him low to keep an anxious watch
    beside.

May'st thou live long to faithfully perform thy marriage
    vow,
And in thy future never know less happiness than now.
May he who sought thee for his bride a worthy consort be,
His little one a bond of love is all I ask for thee.

My kind congratulations on this thy wedding day ;
Best wishes for thy happiness will follow thee away.
Heaven's blessing rest on thee and thine, that when this
    life is past,
He whose love sanctified thy love will give thee joy at
    last.

GO FORTH, MY CHILD.

[FROM A LONG POEM.]

" Within the home domestics slept.   No one
Astir beside the widow and her son,
Grief nearly choked ; yet for his sake,
As if unmoved she calmly spake,
While he in painful attitude,
With his head bowed before her stood."

Go forth, my child, thou must go forth,
              And I who gave thee birth
Must bid thee leave thy childhood's home
              To wander on the earth.

Go hence to some far distant land,
              Where none to censure thee ;
From sins thou canst not here withstand,
              Thou mayest there get free.

Go ; I must not detain thee, howe'er tried ;
              Yet thou must go ;
Though every wish and comfort be denied,
              It must be so.

Leave the dear idol of thy boyhood's love,
          Unworthy her ;
Earth's low debasing vices rise above,
          And good prefer.

Leave the dear girl thou may'st not claim as bride ;
          She'll weep for thee ;
Thy hand love's tender links divide,
          And it must be.

Leave, too, thy mother ; she had hoped for thee
          To watch her life's sunset ;
'Tis sinking quickly down, but it may be
          Thou'll see it yet.

But go, my child, to me thou'rt not less dear,
          Thou hast done ill ;
The prodigal returned, I'll trust nor fear
          God's mercy still.

Guide him, O Father, on the ocean dark
          His journey through ;
Watch o'er his frail and shaky bark,
          Watch o'er him too.

Guard him whene'er temptations strong
          My boy assail ;
Strengthen him, so to flee the wrong
          He may not fail.

Where'er his wandering footsteps stray
             Let nought destroy ;
And in Thy gracious providence one day
             Restore my boy.

Thou hast thy mother's blessings ; now her kiss
             For thee, my son ;
Though hard to separate, to part like this,
             God's will be done.

Farewell, my boy ! away, thou must away,
             For pity's sake ;
If thou dost longer lingering stay,
             My heart will break.

CAPE TOWN, SOUTH AFRICA.

Great mountain range, magnificently grand,
Our eyes beheld thee first when nearing land ;
And, gazing from the deck, we saw
Huge misty wall along the shore.
At daybreak as we steam'd more near,
Thy dark bold outline stood out clear,
Till plain we trac'd along the sky
Each mountain summit towering high.
And as we near and nearer drew
Fresh beauties burst upon our view.
Such I had never seen before,
And view'd thee with admiring awe.
Far as I gazed, my straining eye
Saw thy bold form against the sky,
And at thy feet beheld the spray
Break on the rocks that 'neath thee lay.
And pretty homes and gardens there
Made the fair picture yet more fair.
Small fishing smacks with snowy sail,
Spread out to catch the morning gale,
From out the cove came into view,
And lightly skimm'd the waters blue,
A little fleet of thirty-one,
Sail'd out at rising of the sun.
We slowly steam'd in Table Bay,
The while we there at anchor lay
I looked beyond the busy dock,

Where high above Cape Town—·
Grandly, sublimely, beautiful—
Rose Table Mount's smooth crown,
When on the sea I did admire.
But when upon the land
I stood, surprised, it seem'd to rise
Yet higher—yet more grand ;
My eye was fascinated, quite,
On such a scene to dwell,
My soul's enjoyment in that hour
No pen nor tongue could tell.
Whichever way I looked, my eye
Turn'd with a strange delight,
And rested with what ecstacy
On that bold granite height.
Where pure and bright the waters spring,
And trickle slowly down,
Then into stony basins fall
Midway below the crown.
In tiny, clear, and silvery streams,
Softly murmuring as they go,
Through bushes, over rocks and stones,
Meet in the vale below.
There quite a river—bushes, firs,
Make green the rocky side ;
Stones, boulders spread, forming the bed,
Where the clear waters glide.
Mountain, adieu ; our vessel now
Is steaming from the shore,
Much I regret I cannot yet
Behold thee ; may no more.

HOW SWEET IT IS.

How sweet it is when on a foreign shore,
    Far, far from home, a stranger in the land,
To find a friend in one not seen before,
    And feel the kindly grasp of a warm hand.

How sweet it is when kindred spirits meet,
    When all unconscious thought and feeling blend,
When in the happy hour of converse sweet,
    Each feels the stranger has become a friend.

How sweet it is to feel that tender heart,
    Sorrows and joys like unto thine has known,
That sympathies as quickly from it start
    The while it beats responsive to thine own.

How sweet it is awhile to sit beside
    And gaze into soft eyes where genius glows,
Or with a loving confidence confide
    Some tender secret that none other knows.

How sweet it is the bliss of that calm hour,
    When kindred spirits meet, when smiles and tears,
By looks, not words, express the mighty power
    That makes us feel we've known and lov'd for year

How sweet it is an autograph to see,
    And call to mind the hand that trac'd it here—
Memento of that happy hour when we
    Wish'd that our parting had not been so near.

How sweet it is to know when oceans roll
    Their great, their cold dark barrier between
The heart's affections, nothing can control,
    Nor take from memory joys that once have been.

How sweet it is to know, if never more
    We feel the kindly touch of that warm hand,
One heart responsive beats on that far shore,
    And brings us nearer to that distant land.

ONLY A PICTURE.

Only a picture, but how dear
The sacred hallow'd scene, for here
That grave so distant seems so near

That as I hold it in my hand,
My fancy walks that far-off strand,
And by a dear friend's grave I stand.

Oh, 'tis a privilege to see
That quiet grave, still it will be
A painful happiness to me

To read upon the stone's white face
"In memory of;" his name to trace,
To look on his last resting place,

Where amid strangers and alone
He breath'd his last.   Beneath this stone
Found peace at last before unknown.

Comrades whose hearts beat kind and brave,
In the far bush dug out that grave,
His body honor'd burial gave.

Ah ! they who placed him 'neath the sod,
Knew not how rough the way he trod,
Nor his soul-wrestlings with his God.

I gaze upon the tomb and rail,
And know sin cannot now assail,
But more, I cannot lift the veil.

Sight would not wish to enter in,
For faith can trust beyond to Him
Who died to rescue man from sin.

And one whose heart beat kind and brave,
Has journey'd far across the wave,
Has sought and found that quiet grave ;

Has press'd that turf with silent tread,
Has knelt in prayer above the dead,
Tears of affection o'er him shed.

I thank her for this gift to me,
How valued will the picture be,
Where I that far-off grave can see.

TO A BOY ON THE STEP OF AN OMNIBUS.

I saw thee at the corner, child,
With unkempt hair and look so wild,
And saw thee start as we passed by.
The bus was marked by thy restless eye,
And thou must off to give it chase
With cap in hand and eager face.
Now other urchins with thee run,
What street boy can resist the fun
All are soon tired out save thee,
Yet thou dost run though faint must be ;
Thy limbs will fail thee yet I fear,
And thou not win and yet so near.
Ah! no, thy hand the step has caught,
Thou hast not persevered for nought.
Be seated, thou hast won the seat,
Rest thy poor tired, shoeless feet ;
Now wipe thy face so hot and red,
Place the old cap upon thy head,
With such a happy look of pride,
Contented with thy humble ride.
What a triumphant look to cast
At those who could not run so fast.
But why at me that look of fear?
Art wondering if foes be near ?
Will the whip sting thy half-clad form ?
Or the old cap from thy head be torn ?

I could not drive thee from thy seat,
So hardly earn'd and such a treat.
But here we part, thy journey o'er,
For thee no need to open door,
No fare to take, one skilful bound,
Thou'rt off and standing on the ground.
I shall not soon forget thy run,
But, farewell, little nameless one.

A SEASIDE SKETCH.

[FROM A LONG POEM.]

The setting sun has crimsoned the sky o'er Holdfast Bay,
Beneath so calm and still the sparkling waters lay ;
The tiny waves but ripple, scarcely more,
And softly murmuring kiss the sandy shore.
The hour when crowds of people flock to promenade the
      pier,
From fashionable hotel, from every dwelling near ;
Worn out with the heat of a long summer's day,
They seek the beach or jetty and long past midnight stay ;
Or row in little dingeys about the waters bright,
For what is more enjoyable than boating by moonlight ?
A widow lady slowly walks, a stripling by her side,
Though a mere child, so tenderly he seems her steps to
      guide.
He is carrying a book and campstool in his hand,
The latter he soon fixes for his mother on the sand ;
She, feeling very weary, rests thankful on the seat,
He rests himself upon the sand recumbent at her feet ;
They view the lovely scene—far, far, the waters lie,
Now quiet and serene 'neath the golden sunlit sky—
And wonder how the ocean can stoutest hearts alarm,
Rise in such awful fury yet sink to such sweet calm.
They heavenward silent gaze. An Australian sun's jus
      set ;

Whose eye that glorious sight beholds methinks can ne'er
  forget.
The golden clouds above in lovely form and figure rise,
Like castles and cathedrals grand or thrones set in the
  skies.
The while they silent gaze on the illumin'd sky,
Seeming too beautifully grand, dazzling to mortal eye,
They feel a sacred awe as if to them is given
To see beyond this world of care the distant gate of
  heaven.
They watch the crowd of people moving along the pier,
When a young girl from among them seems to be drawing
  near ;
Her presence brings a happy smile across the lady's face,
The youth has marked her coming and risen from his
  place.
He gathers up some seaweed and for her makes a seat ;
They then recline together just at the lady's feet,
And chat with all the freedom of older friends, and yet,
'Tis but a week or two ago since on the beach they met.
They love the quiet ocean beyond the city's din,
And watch the waves stretch farther—the tide is flowing
  in.

" Let's write our names upon the sand,
And see whose will the longer stand ;
Here goes mine first, now Ethel you
Must write your own above it, do !
My mother's next I'll write it here,
Just beside ours but not too near ;
Should the waves come up very strong,
And roughly wash the sand along,

They'll very soon our names erase,
Nor leave behind the slightest trace ;
But if they gently break away,
You'll see we shall a long time stay ;
It is such fun I wonder whether
We'll all go out to sea together."

The waters quickly near their feet,
And higher up he took the seat ;
Then rough and strong the white waves came,
Washing around young Clifford's name ;
Running small streamlets in between,
Then over and 'twas no more seen.

The widow's name washed next away.
" Why, Ethel, do they let you stay ?
'Tis strange the waters leave you here,
When I and mother were as near ;
They might have let me by you stay,
Or taken both of us away.

But Ethel, darling, never mind,
In future fate will be more kind."

The widow on the children smile,
But she is deep in thought the while ;
Praying the sea will ne'er divide
Her and the dear ones now beside.

Life has its changes dark with care,
Its storm-clouds gather everywhere ;
But happy childhood little dreams
Life is less sunny than it seems.

The pier is getting crowded, the beach is quite alive,
Still all kinds of vehicles continue to arrive ;

Bearing the young, the aged too, all glad to leave the
    city,
The cripple and the invalid so much deserving pity.
Some scarce can reach the seats, fainting for air and rest,
Others yet young and full of life think promenading best;
While couples who are fortunate and gain a sheltered
    seat,
Are by themselves indulging in a sly flirtation sweet;
And children, merry children, their laughter ringing loud,
With hat in hand are chasing one another through the
    crowd.

While lovers in yon little boat
Upon the placid waters float;
Rounding the jetty head, they glide
Away far off the other side;
Past groups of bathers near to shore;
Then rest awhile the dripping oar,
Just off Merino's pebbly coast;
Less frequented they like it most,
Where all around so calm and still,
The little boat may move at will.

The sea so peaceful, scarce a wave
Breaks where the tide the dark rocks lave.
The moon's bewitching, silvery light
Making a glittering pathway bright
Across the ocean to the sky.

Beyond the ken of mortal eye,
Bound by the spell of that bright moon,
Hand linked in hand, in soul commune,
They on the lovely waters gaze,
And dream of bliss in coming days.

Soul·stirring scene when none is near !
The lover in his maiden's ear
Pours forth again his tale of love,
Vows constancy by all above ;
Impulsive grasps his idle oar,
And pulls again along the shore.

IN MEMORIAM, DR. BAYER.

Death, death has claimed thee, noble one,
Alas, thy too short life is done.
Physician of exalted skill
Thy place who can so ably fill?
Each noble thought, each hour of time
Were given to thy work sublime.
Of iron nerve thou wert possessed,
To torture when thou deem'd it best.
No summer's heat, no winter's rain
E'er kept thee from the bed of pain.
How many now around us stand
Snatched from the grave by thy strong hand.
To thee how often did we feel
Christ had vouchsafed the power to heal,
And see as o'er the past we scan
Thou lived but for thy brother man.
In thy profession thy life was spent,
Thou died its brightest ornament.
Kind man, beloved by rich and poor,
All, all lament thou art no more.
When sick we'll wish for thee in vain,
Thou never more may'st come again.
'Twere vain to raise our weary head
We shall not hear thy welcome tread.
When thou wert by whom all loved much,
Than thine not gentler woman's touch.

If there was hope thy tender voice
Did speak it and with us rejoice ;
And when, alas, no hope thou gave
We felt no human skill could save.
When gloomy feelings o'er us crept
Kind one thou wept with us who wept.
Alas, it came thy hour to go,
The great physician was laid low.
Unconscious thou kind friends stood by
Breathing a prayer thou might not die.
Each noble thought of thy busy brain
Was clouded never to work again.
Thou could'st not give one farewell smile,
They watch'd in cruel suspense awhile ;
No farewell word by thee was said,
A few short hours, the loved friend was dead.

THE SECOND GRIEF.

Sleep, little infant, sleep, I would not waken thee ;
I would not thou could'st share the grief which seems too
    much for me.
Sleep, little infant, sleep, thou know'st not o'er thee
    bends
A heart aching for thee, thy tenderest of friends.
I grieve not for thee now ; God's will is best—'tis done.
But gazing on thy lifeless form I think again of one
Who died but yesterday it seems, and left my side for
    ever.
Thou wert a tiny living link, keeping us close together ;
A little gift remaining, something he left behind.
I loved to cherish for the sake of one so true and kind,
Whose eyes with father's love so fondly on thee smiled ;
Who planned a glorious future when thou had'st outgrown
    the child ;
Whose gentle hands once fondled and lifted on his knee.
Part of his very self, as such I nurtured thee.
Fair picture of thy father, so lifelike ; I could trace
Almost his every feature in thy little baby face ;
So like him even now in this death's cold repose.
I wonder art thou with him? alas ! God only knows.
Christ, who made little children His own especial care,
Bade thee to follow Him.   I would unmurmuring spare.
I tasted then this bitter cup, drank deep, but did not
    drain.
Again I raise it to my lips, for yet the dregs remain.

Yes, since it is Thy will, so let Thy will be done.
Yes, Thou may'st have him too ; sleep on, my little one.
Upon thy placid brow not a sign of sin thine own ;
There might have been how many had'st thou to man-
hood grown—
I would have done my best to keep thee in the narrow
way ;
But midst the world's temptations thou might have gone
astray.
Then, while so young and sinless, it was good of Thee, O
God,
To gently break the golden bowl, and loose life's silver
cord.

WINTER'S COMING IN ENGLAND.

Now the stripping east winds blow,
    Trees are looking sere and bare ;
And the clouds of brown leaves go,
    Dancing through the chilly air.

Once I watched for joyous spring-time,
    For the bright green buds to burst ;
Waited for the bright warm sunshine,
    And green leaves I hailed the first.

Soon the country grew so charming,
    Hill and dale and cornfields green ;
In the fields when harvest gathered,
    Merry children ran to glean.

Next I heard the swallows twitter,
    As they met at early morn,
Laid their plans for emigrating,
    Winter's coming—they are gone.

Autumn tints so bright, so lovely,
    Decking hedge-row, wood, and wall,
Beautiful as summer blossoms,
    Winter's coming—fast ye fall.

Bleak winds blow and thick fogs gather,
    Soon will come hoar-frost and snow ;
Back to our warm sunny island,
    Winter's coming, let us go.

ON A FRIEND'S ENGAGEMENT.

Well I know that jewelled circlet
 On thy finger is the token
Of thy young heart's pure affection,
 Of loves' vows so fond'y spoken.

Loving words so softly whispered,
 Found response in thy warm heart ;
Tenderly those vows were uttered,
 Binding each till death doth part.

He has woo'd thee, he has won thee,
 Would thee all his future share ;
Now I ask of God above thee,
 Shield and bless this happy pair.

Grant that nought disturb thy friendship,
 Nought may mar thy heart's delight ;
Bless your souls in mystic union,
 Shield when marriage bonds unite.

Loved one, I congratulate thee,
 In thy happiness rejoice,
May God grant all earthly blessings
 To thee and thy young heart's choice.

Still, methinks, I see thy finger,
 With its sacred jewelled sign ;
And fond fancy yet will linger,
 Picturing happiness like thine.

MARRIAGE LINES.

Hail, happy day ! dear friend, thou'st watch'd its dawning,
With hope and fear to greet thy bridal morning ;
Thy vows will soon be spoken, the holy knot be tied :
United, loving bridegroom, with his young trusting bride.

Thy father's blessing be with thee, dear friend—
Thy mother's blessing from above descend ;
And He who all hearts' secrets doth reveal,
Bless thee when thou dost at His altar kneel.

And when thou dost arise, made man and wife,
May He protect and guide thy future life ;
So shall love's promises be kept aright,
And thou walk worthily in Heaven's sight.

" To have and to hold," in mystic bond united
For life, till death do part, thy troth is plighted ;
" For better for worse," in sickness and in health,
'Mid poverty's cares or the glories of wealth.

Thy partner, dear friend, may he prove
A husband worthy woman's love ;
Living a life, so when it's past,
Thou'lt share one blessed home at last.

To wish thee joy I fain would longer stay,
Still more to feel than I had power to say—
Bright be thy future, scarcely dimm'd by care,
God bless thee, friend, God bless thee, happy pair.

GOING HOME.

Upon the deck my rug is spread, and prostrate here I lie,
Watching the tiny snow-white clouds that cross the bright
    blue sky ;
Listening to the waves that break against the vessel's sides,
Watching the stately albatross as gracefully he glides,
Or rests upon blue-crested wave, then skims majestically
On wide-spread wing our vessel round, then far away to
    sea.
Free wanderer thou, tell ! tell to me where, whither dost
    thou roam ?
Say if upon this watery waste thou now art going home ?

Say, when the sun has sunk to rest, when darkness clouds
    the sky,
When cold night winds are howling round and billows
    rolling high,
When land birds 'neath their weary wing have placed
    their head to rest,
Wilt thou, like them upon the shore, have found a cosy
    nest ?
Some reef where breakers dash around, washed by the
    angry foam,
Perchance where mighty billows roar thou lovest to make
    thy home.

Where hast thou been, what hast thou seen? thy wandering career
Has led thee oft 'mid storms and strife, without a thought
  of fear ;
Where lightning flashed round creaking mast, and
  deafening thunder pealed,
When the sea rose in mad fury and the strong-built vessel
  reeled.
What hast thou heard of shrieks and prayers when far
  upon the foam ?
Brave hearts have sank beneath the wave as they were
  going home !

Going home ! how do those simple words suggest grave
  thoughts to me ;
You doubtless, noble bird, have home somewhere upon
  the sea.
We sail upon the boundless deep across the ocean wide,
And hope ere many weeks have passed to reach the other
  side ;
And think of friends we parted from to cross the ocean's
  foam,
Of many more we long to see—for we are going home.

Alas, among us there is one consumption's marked for
  prey
Who prostrate lies upon his couch all through each weary
  day,
So young, yet nevermore will he across the ocean sail ;

We fear lest ere he reach the shore our brother's strength
will fail,
So young in pride of manhood yet he soon will cease to
roam,
Will leave this world, but oh ! we trust that he is Going
Home.

DEDICATED TO ——————— AT THEIR

JUBILEE WEDDING.

Hail, worthy pair ! whose Golden Wedding Day
We meet to celebrate, and honour pay.
Exampled in whose loving constancy
The blessedness of marriage do we see.
Fifty long, useful, happy years have sped
Since ye in spring-time of bright hopes were wed.
How many a year of anxious toil and care,
Lived out by patient strength and fervent prayer,
To wisdom, love, and virtue both inclined
In blessed singleness of heart and mind ;
In true companionship of man and wife,
Ye've stood the trial great of human life.
By diligence, by firm, unflagging zeal,
Have sought your own and many another's weal,
Favoured by God and honoured among men.
Both lives stretch back o'er threescore years and ten.
Old age approaches with considerate touch ;
Nor health nor energy impaireth much.
Memory is sweet, unmarred by aught of pain.
Time has but rivetted love's golden chain.
Your favoured children seek to imitate
And follow after parents good and great.
Six are permitted round you here to stand,
And four are waiting in that "better land."

O'er life's tempestuous sea so long ye've sailed,
Your chart, the Bible, guiding ne'er has failed
To point to that last blessed port of call,
Where sin and death no longer shall appal.
To love and to be loved may God long spare
The dear, dear objects of His love and care.

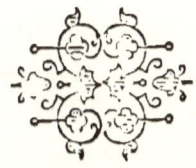

HOMEWARD BOUND.

Oh ! when out of harbour our vessel is steaming,
  Away from Old England, our dear native land,
I watch till no longer bright coast lights are gleaming,
  And the night winds blow cold on the deck where we
    stand;
When we look for the dear ones no longer around,
One thought only cheering the thought — Homeward
  Bound.

I shall never forget thee, Old England—no, never !
  The land of my birth, so lately my home,
Where friends warmly welcom'd me—dearer than ever
  Thou art now and will be wherever I roam ;
When I gaze on the dark waters splashing around
I shall yet sigh for England e'en though Homeward
  Bound.

Forget thee, my country, could any forget thee?
  Cathedral and abbey each wonderful scene ;
Forget all thy glories ; ah ! no, ever let me
  In fancy re-visit each spot where I've been ;
From thee, from the many kind friends I have found
I could not away, but we're now Homeward Bound.

Ah ! beautiful England, where loved ones are dwelling,
  Whose home was my home when I visited thee ;

With mingled emotions my bosom is swelling,
 For dear ones await me far over the sea.
In yon bright sunny isle no place have I found
More dear to my heart, and we're now Homeward Bound.

Then Old England farewell, farewell hoar frost and snow,
 I go where the orange and citron trees grow,
Where grapes in rich clusters are bending the vine,
 Where are blue cloudless skies and dazzling sunshine,
And range after range of bold hills stretching round ;
Oh my heart leaps for joy at the thought Homeward
  Bound.

" Merry Christmas " in England with relatives dear,
 With feastings, rejoicings, we'll hail the New Year :
Then grieve not too sadly, dear ones, in your hearts
 When out of the harbour our vessel departs,
But think when ye gather your bright firesides round
The loved ones you miss are away Homeward Bound.

INTEMPERANCE.

Intemperance, what fell destroyer thou !
To thee the young, the hoary-headed bow ;
None are too great for thee to overthrow,
None too exalted, thou can'st bring all low.
Earth's noblest, brightest-gifted, fall a prey
To thee, and from the path of wisdom stray.
Thou'rt ever seeking whom thou may'st devour,
Whom thou may'st crush by thy debasing power ;
Dividing brothers, sisters, man and wife,
Till happy homes become abodes of strife ;
Blighting fair prospects, sullying proudest name,
Checking the youthful aspirant to fame ;
The clever boy, the child of gentle birth,
Becomes a homeless wanderer on the earth—
A slave to thee ! beyond friends' power to save,
He dies unwept, and fills a drunkard's grave.
Nought is too good for thy rude touch to spoil,
E'en purity's white robes thy foul stains soil :
Thou hast no mercy, for thou dost not spare
The gentle maiden, virtuous and fair,
Till robb'd of all once dear, but thee to blame,
She lives a life of dissipation—shame !
Intemperance ! alas, man know'st well,
How many a soul by thee condemn'd to hell.
How many a parent's heart thou'st wrung with grief,
How many a lifetime hast made all too brief,

How many sent to an unhallow'd grave ;
Thy victims numberless, whom none could save,
Thy curse, thy cruel deeds we daily see.
O would that man would strive to conquer thee !
Would warn and guard the young ere they begin
To love thee ! first—then every other sin.

AN INVALID'S DEATH.

Death has taken yet another of the dear ones whom we
    love
From this world of dreary darkness, to that brighter
    world above;
She was one on whom our Father early laid the chas-
    tening rod,
But who questioned not nor murmured at the discipline of
    God.

We shall not miss her in the halls where pride and
    fashion meet,
Where the young and lovely linger, deeming trifling
    pleasures sweet;
Nor where earth's great and gifted are straining nerve
    and brain
To reach ambition's dizzy height, and win earth's glory
    vain.

We shall miss her where she passed each sad and weary
    day,
At home where stands the vacant couch on which she
    lately lay;
Where we've seen her writhe in agony, and exhausted
    sink to sleep,
And shrinking from all she endured, have turned aside
    to weep.

Or, when rebellious feelings made our lot seem hard to
  bear,
Looking on that sweet, patient face our murmur turned
  to prayer.
She was waiting, calmly waiting, till the call from earth
  was given,
Longing to join the ransomed throng, and sing the songs
  of heaven.

It came—the angels whispered the dear Redeemer's call ;
She joyfully obeyed, leaving parents, friends, and all ;
Laying down life's heavy cross, she bade farewell to
  earthly strife,
And slept the peaceful sleep of death—to wake to
  endless life.

There was no shrinking at the last, when life and death
  were met ;
Few sins to be repented of, few errors to regret ;
Save the love of aged parents, brothers and sisters dear,
Save the sweet ties of kindred, there was nought to hold
  her here.

Her form we grieved to look on will be raised a perfect
  thing ;
Her head be crowned with glory, her voice triumphan
  sing.
We have laid her in the tomb, there nought can break
  her rest ;
But her soul is with its Saviour, with the redeemed and
  blest.

WELCOME TO AN INFANT.

Welcome, sweet babe, ah ! who can know
Thy blessed mission here below.
May'st thou in safety tread the path of life,
Kept undefiled amid its care and strife ;
Joyous and simple light of heart and mild,
The sunshine of thy happy home, fair child.
In childhood's days God bless and prosper thee,
And make thee all a woman ought to be,
A joy, a comfort in the midst of strife,
To some who feel the burden of this life.
Mid dark'ning shades of sorrow and of care,
A joy, a hope, a comfort everywhere.
Whatever sphere of life destined to fill,
Labouring in love to do thy Father's will ;
And parents, friends, who thank'd God thou wert
    giv'n,
Be all one family at last in Heaven.

THE YOUNG PASTOR'S WIFE.

She sat upon the vessel's deck,
  So late a blushing bride,
But where, where is her young heart's choice,
  Why parted from her side ?

To foreign lands he went away,
  There to prepare a home,
Now anxious waits each weary day
  Her coming o'er the foam.

A placid smile is on her face,
  A face unmark'd by care,
O what more lovely to behold
  Than woman chaste and fair.

She sat apart, we worked or read,
  But ofttimes from my book
My eyes would stray that other way,
  On her sweet face to look.

To read her soul methought I'd power
  As with a steadfast gaze
She scanned the sea at twilight's hour
  And thought of coming days.

Affection pure had link'd those two ;
  Gay gallants linger'd by—
Each flattering word, as if unheard,
  Pass'd her unheeded by.

They leave her side—'tis silent eve,
  Far o'er the peaceful sea—
She looks, fond thoughts her heart relieve,
  Her musings such to me.

To aid thee in thy Master's work
  Shall be life's noble aim,
A share of all thy hopes and fears
  My privilege to claim.

Beside the sick to watch and pray,
  To seek out sore distress,
Illumining with heavenly ray
  Dark homes of wretchedness.

To visit, too, the widow lone,
  The fatherless and poor,
To teach Christ where He is not known,
  His name unheard before.

Great blessèd work before us now—
  She moves her lips to pray ;
My Father give us grace that we
  Exalt Thy name alway.

She starts—a look almost of pain—
  Sounds of unseemly mirth
Have roused her from her happy dream—
  Brought back her thoughts to earth.

How oft will memory fondly trace
  Mid busy scenes of life,
That brow serene, the angel face,
  Of that young pastor's wife.

AT REST FOR EVER.

LINES PRESENTED TO THE SCHOLARS OF ST.
AUGUSTINE'S SUNDAY SCHOOL, UNLEY, ON THE
DEATH OF THEIR SUPERINTENDENT.

Now at rest, at rest for ever, after weary toil and strife,
Christian soldier fallen nobly on the battle-field of life ;
Now the weary march is ended, and the bitter conflict
    done,
Now the victor's crown of glory with immortal life is won.

Now at rest, at rest for ever. Oh ! how many thou hast
    taught
The way of life—how many wanderers nearer to the
    Saviour brought ;
In the hearts of little children sown first seeds of love and
    truth,
By kind council cheer'd the aged, won the heedless,
    erring'youth.

Now at rest, at rest for ever, thou wilt ne'er keep watch
    again
By the bedside of the dying, by the weary couch of pain ;
Mourn'd by this world's great and wealthy, by the poor
    thou hast befriended,
By the flock that's lost the shepherd who so long and
    kindly tended.

Now at rest, at rest for ever, low is laid thy tired head,
And we mourn a friend, a brother, sleeping in his narrow
bed.
Thou hast left us, thou hast conquered all of painfulness
and strife,
Left this dark world for that brighter, and its sinless,
endless life.

Now at rest, at rest for ever, hearts are full and eyes are
wet,
All thy kind, unceasing labour while on earth we'll not
forget ;
Comfort sweet, the Spirit saith, " Blessed are the dead
which die
In the Lord, they rest for ever, dwell in immortality."

Now at rest, at rest for ever, tender husband, parent kind,
And with feeling hearts we sorrow with bereaved ones
left behind.
In the hour when fond hearts breaking, feel home's
dearest ties are riven,
May the Father's grace sustain them, lead them in thy
steps to Heaven.

Now at rest, at rest for ever.   Little children, wherefore
weep ?
Know ye not your dear, kind teacher is not dead, but
gone to sleep ?
Parted for a little season, hidden for a while from view,
In those mansions Christ prepared, now he waits to welcome you.

Dry your tears, ye youthful mourners, he would not that
    ye should mourn ;
Live according to his teachings, follow on where he has
    gone ;
Cull earth's choicest, sweetest flowers, strew them o'er
    the hallowed sod,
Where the good man's dust reposes, while his spirit lives
    with God.

TO —— ON LEAVING TASMANIA.

I wish thee farewell, since farewel! it must be,
But know that I'll often be thinking of thee—
Of our long stay in Hobart, each beautiful spot
It has been ours to visit will ne'er be forgot ;
How much we enjoy'd the cool bracing weather ;
Oft walked by the side of the Derwent together,
Or choosing its smooth, grassy bank for a seat
Watch'd the play of the dancing waves at our feet ;
On the Esplanade wandered or rested at ease,
Enjoying the view and the health-giving breeze ;
Wistfully gazing across the blue bay
Where stately warships at anchor lay,
Where graceful yachts o'er the waters glide,
And sunlit hills gleam on the further side ;
* Have steamed far out to that lonesome shore,
Where the angry billows make deafening roar,
Scaled high rocks where the tide had just been,
Leapt o'er deep chasms which intervene ;
Trodden along narrow ledges of rock,
The sea our trespassing seeming to mock ;
Stoop'd low 'neath the vaulted roof overhead,
Seen the angry waves in their deep, dark bed,
Where the spirit of storm had been brought to play
On the mighty mass till it forced its way

---

* The celebrated Blow Hole on the coast of Tasman's Peninsula
the Steamer Monarch making an excursion trip in the season.

Through stupendous rock to the other side,
Forming a tunnel both long and wide ;
Mountain-high billows came rolling in,
With a fearful crash, like artillery's din ;
Together gazed in reverent thought,
Spell-bound at Neptune's terrible sport,
As the breakers dashed high the foaming spray,
Leaving mimic waterfalls on their way.
Have climbed Mount Wellington ; from its crown
On the vast panorama we looked down.
Mountains, rivers, and sea with irregular beach,
Repeated oft, far as the eye could reach ;
Bright shone old Sol, we entranc'd tarried there,
Till warned to descend by the keen Alpine air,
Our four-in-hand reach'd in soil'd terrible plight,
As Mount Wellington's cap was donned for the night.
Fair, fair was each scene, but, oh, fairer to me,
That its beauties were shared with companions like
        thee.
Perhaps not for years, but oh, not in vain,
May we cherish the hope of yet meeting again.

BUCKS, ENGLAND.

Beautiful country ! while visiting here,
Beholding each spot of interest near,
Have our eyes grown familiar with each lovely scene—
With fields of ripe grain, and meadow land green.
"Great Shardeloes Park," where we loved to take
A stroll 'neath the elms by the side of the lake ;
Or under tall beeches our way slowly wend,
Past game preserves, over the stile, to "Mop End."

Long drives on bright days I shall never forget ;
By each pleasant way memory's leading me yet.
To West Wycombe Church on the top of the hill,
Where we rambled about, or rested at will ;
From the ball of the tower—rare, beautiful sight—
O'er the country afar my eye ranged with delight.
The damp, gloomy caves, where we shivered with cold ;
Their chalk walls lit up was a sight to behold.

Little gem of a church that at Chesham Bois,
On the hillside, removed far from bustle and noise.
We climbed up the hill, where the wind blew so strong,
So bracing and fresh as we journeyed along ;
And blackberries hung so invitingly black,
To gather we tarried, or turned a step back.
The plain, hearty service I'll never forget,
Where few save the humblest together were met.

The bright afternoon when on pleasure intent,
With baskets equipped, all blackberrying went;
Through a wood to "Wood Row," so abundant they
    grew,
We soon filled the baskets, and wanted more too;
Where berries hung thickest no need for to tell
That briars and brambles protected them well.

Our walks in the wood, where at every turn
Grew beautiful beeches, bright mosses, and fern;
Where around all so wildly luxuriant grew,
The bright sky above was most hidden from view.
The stile where we rested sometimes half an hour,
Beside field of rich clover in bright purple flower;
Below us the old town of Amersham lay,
And the river ran, turning old mills on its way;
The church's grey tower and burying ground too
Of hillside and valley—most beautiful view!

AN ENGLISH VILLAGE CHURCHYARD
SCENE.

An ancient little village church ; around it many graves,
With crumbling headstones, broken rails—o'er some the
    green grass waves.
Upon its walls and towers grey old Time has left his
    trace,
For moss and ivy seem to love the quiet hallowed place.

Yon gray haired man has sought this spot—here his
    ancestors lay—
An old man now; in foreign parts he long has dwelt away.
Again beside his mother's grave 'tis granted him to stand,
Again to meet his kindred in his dear fatherland.

To him, that grave close by the church the dearest spot
    on earth ;
There lies the dust of woman loved, of her who gave him
    birth ;
And, standing by, the past returns.   How many years have
    fled
Since one among the sorrowing throng he follow'd the
    dead.

More than quarter of a century of changeful years have
    flown.
He has returned, and once again he stands beside that
    stone ;

Change and decay mark all around, yet the loved spot he
knew,
The ivy clinging to the wall beside the same old yew.

But his no gloomy sorrow as he mourns the loved ones
dead,
Over the memory of the past no bitter tears he shed ;
His is such grief as worthy son can only feel, when he
Returns, after the lapse of years, his parents' grave to see.

"Life's bitter scene of toil is o'er," those words again he
read,
Raising his eyes to heaven where he knew her spirit fled.
Dear, sacred spot ! his mother's grave he nevermore will
see,
And silently he moved away, so sad at heart was he.

No, nevermore ! he turned again to look for the last time,
For he had made another home in a distant sunny clime ;
But memory oft will bring him back to that dear
cherished spot—
His grandsire's and his mother's grave will never be
forgot.

DEATH'S NARRATION.

I was where a pale young woman drew near with noiseless
    tread
And gently raised the covering from off a little bed.
She stooped and gazed, with anguish I saw her bosom
    throb,
Lower she bent.   I heard a kiss, and then a stifled sob,
And hovering near beheld her grief.   I knew what made
    her weep—
She was a mother, there her child lay still in his last long
    sleep.
She loved him much ; I deemed it sport to rend those
    loving ties,
The dearest idol of her heart to shatter before her eyes.
I stayed with my withering touch his breath,
And the thing she loved most was cold in death.
Mounting my white horse I sped, till I found
A manly figure stretched out on the ground,
With broken limbs and bleeding wounds in fearful pain
    he lie,
A victim of dissipation.   Why should I pass him by?
I saw his handsome features now dull and ghastly grown,
And heard the fearful oath that passed his lips with every
    moan.
I'd passed him when a gentle youth he'd run a sinful
    course ;
Deluded soul, deep plunged in vice, he seldom felt
    remorse.

Into the soul of many a one he had corruption poured,

Nor thought how soon he was to face a deeply injured
God.

His mother's prayers unheeded, his Bible cast aside,

His burning lips now parted in agony he cried,

And called on me to ease his pain, his deeply tortured
mind—

Cried, " Had'st thou found me when a boy, Death, thou
had'st been more kind."

No longer I stayed for his painful gaze, nor heeded his
piteous cry,

But taking my brand I stamped his brow and left him
thus to die.

Away from that sickening scene I rode and, just at dawn
of day,

Drew rein at a splendid mansion and thought there awhile
to stay.

I found prostrate upon a couch a young and lovely girl,

Her small thin fingers listlessly played with her golden
curl.

I hovered o'er such beauty, her patient smile to see ;

She was worthy a place in Paradise, she felt no fear of
me.

I listened to dear friends who prayed she might have
longer life,

And heard the stifled sob of he who knelt by his promised
wife.

She was so good, so pure, so frail, for me it seemed but
kind

To loose life's silver cord and let her leave the world
behind,

So, placing my icy hand on her brow, cut short her trem-
　　bling breath,
Sealed her lips with my fatal kiss, closed her bright eyes
　　in death.

To the youthful, the aged, I fain would say,
Prepare for my coming, you know not the day.
I'm seeking for prey as I pass to and fro,
None know when I come nor whither I go.
I've a work to accomplish which cannot be o'er
Till such time as time itself is no more.

THE MEMORY OF THE PAST.

The memory of the past comes flitting through my brain,
And pathways trodden long ago I'm treading once again ;
The voices, too, of loved ones are ringing in mine ear,
The very gloamings peopled with forms of the absent dear.

The memory of the past, how potent is thy spell !
How sweetly soothing thy soft influence ! too mystical
    to tell.
To feel the past brought near again is dearer far to me
Than to gaze into the future if 'twere given me to see.

The memory of the past has much to cheer us yet,
Although sometimes the heart will have some feelings of
    regret.
I would not linger o'er the past only to cull its flowers ;
There are thorns enough, God only knows, in this present
    life of ours.

When the heart knows its own bitterness, the world seems
    full of care ;
'Tis the memory of the past has power to keep us from
    despair,
To sound the battle-cry recalling soldiers, gone before,
Who were valiant in life's conflict—crown'd and resting
    evermore.   ,

As darkest nights of storm and strife give place to brightest
    morn,
So life has its cares and pleasures, and crosses must be
    borne ;
O never feel down-hearted ; all encouragement may find,
If they but trace their Father's love in pathways left
   behind.

Yes, the memory of the past to the present lends a charm,
And upon the wounded spirit pours some healing balm ;
Bids the heart forget its trouble, awhile be light and free,
O the memory of the past is a source of joy to me.

ON THE BIRTH OF THE FIRSTBORN.

Methinks that I can see thee lie
   So peacefully at rest,
Thine arm around the angel babe
   That's nestling at thy breast.

A look of satisfaction trace
   Upon thy youthful brow,
A happy smile of holy joy ;
   Thou art a mother now.

Thine own, that little angel form,
   One of the Saviour's lambs ;
Thine own to shield from earthly storm,
   To tend with loving hands.

God's given thee thy heart's desire,
   Thou hast thy little one ;
O may He long be pleased to spare
   Thee, mother, and thy son.

I bid thee welcome, little one,
   With warmest love I do ;
Parents with joy have hail'd thy birth,
   I bid thee welcome too.

At what a gentle mother's breast,
   Babe, thou wilt nourished be ;
There little cherub calmly rest,
   Tis pure, how fit for thee.

Sweet babe, thy earliest infant gaze
   Shall seek a father's face,
Where manhood in its noblest form,
   Thou there may truly trace.

Thus reared within a happy home,
   Where rests God's holy love,
Thy earliest, purest, childish thoughts
   Shall rise to Him above.

God guard thy boyhood then,
   And may thy manhood be
A blessing to thy parents.
   May God bless them and thee.

HAPPY IS HE.

Happy is he on England's shore to stand,
  Who absent many, many years has been,
Who visits once again his native land,
  And fondly looks on each familiar scene.

And grasps the hand of old friends left behind,
  When years ago he sought a foreign shore ;
Feels that their hearts beat still as true and kind,
  There friendship is as hearty as of yore.

Ah ! none can know such happiness save he
  Who leaves his kindred and his fatherland ;
Crosses o'er thousands miles of dreary sea,
  And founds a new home on a foreign strand.

Where not one soul to give him hearty cheer,
  He bears the heat and burden of the day ;
Toils for his partner and his children dear,
  Till fortune smiling sheds a brighter ray.

When, after many years of active toil,
  Through exercise of firm unflagging zeal,
He stands once more upon his native soil,
  And feels a pleasure others cannot feel.

IN MEMORIAM.

I gazed upon thy wasted form by suffering sorely tried,
And thought, but two years since, thou wert a happy
bride ;
No lines of care and sorrow then were traced upon thy
brow,
Where the cold sweat stands thick death rests in triumph
now.

The tiny babe thou fondly hoped to nourish at thy
breast
Is left without a mother now, since thou art gone to rest.
Thy husband, parents, sisters, friends, thou hast left
sorrowing here,
And gone the way of the earth, gone for ever, sister dear.

Thou hast trodden the rough pathway, that fearful
dark unknown,
And we must follow soon although thou went'st first
alone.
Thou'rt gone before, my sister dear, oh, while we here do
stay,
May each of us prepare for heaven as thou hast shown the
way.

Thy sufferings that on earth were great, in heaven we
know are o'er,
For we trust thou art gone to where thy Saviour pass'd
before ;

And while we gaze upon thy form the solemn truth but
     trace,
We've "no continuing city here" and "no abiding place."

To night I pressed my trembling lips upon thy clammy
     brow,
But felt I could not wish thee back, for thou art happy
     now.
Though short thy stay among us, ere thy work on earth
     was done,
Death lost its sting by thee, through faith death's terrors
     were o'ercome.

Thy closèd eyes and folded hands methinks I see them
     now,
What perfect peace was written upon thy noble brow ;
It pleasèd God to take thee ; oh, that we every one
Could meekly bow beneath the stroke and say " Thy will
     be done."

OUR HOLIDAY RIDE.

(BY REQUEST OF ONE OF THE PARTY.)

The ninth day of November, and such a charming day,
But a few clouds at early morn and they passing away,
When seated at our breakfast a knock came at the door.
"What early callers; hark! it's Tom and Harry, I feel
    sure."
They come to see, if disengaged, with them we'll take a
    ride ;
'Tis fine, so Nell and I in the affirmative replied.
We've but one saddle horse at home, but near by have a
    friend,
Who rides a splendid creature and has offered it to lend.
A note the man has taken, his return I scarce can wait,
But looking through the field-glass, fix upon Barn Abbey
    Gate.
He comes—Bob on our Gipsy, I'm sure, too—I am
    right.
He leads a prancing palfrey, with saddle cloth of white.
The clouds are passing off, the sky is bright and clear,
'Tis time we some refreshment take, our friends will soon
    be here.
And what a charming breeze is blowing off the sea,
A day more suited for our ride I'm sure there could not be
Our habits donned, our cavaliers will be arriving soon.
The sound of horses' hoofs approach, we were to start at
    noon ;
The horses all stand ready, they are a handsome four,

Neither appear too steady, we'll quiet them, I'm sure.
My Gipsy's eye is on me, she frets to get away,
Our ride of five-and-twenty miles will be to her but play;
But yonder little coal black steed with eye flashing like
    fire,
Will bear me on as rapidly, but will it sooner tire?
It stands a perfect picture, so lightly built and sound,
With head erect, as restlessly it stamps and paws the
    ground.

Nelly is in her saddle, Harry has followed suit,
I mount my little charger, and Tom his powerful brute.
We're off—my pony's restive, we for a canter start,
One bound, away flies Tom, we company must part;
'Twere wrong to follow on, my pony back I hold.
I trust his horse is safe, it's hard to be controlled,
It seems a vicious brute, see how he grasps the rein.
His horsemanship is faulty, out of practice it is plain.
The dusty town is reached, soon it is left behind
Our horses' heads turned toward the hills a purer breeze
    we find.

Up ride the other two, we take a little rest
Indulging in a laugh at Tom while riding all abreast.
Nelly enjoys her ride, look at her happy face;
Dear girl, how well she looks, and sits her horse with
    grace.
Her companion's rather quiet, just the reverse is mine,
His face all animation, with fun his bright eyes shine.
Before we'd ridden far, he said, "Some verses you must
    write
About to-day."   "Oh, very well, but mind you must
    indite;

If I see aught to write about I will with all my heart.
Are you disposed to break your neck and play a hero's
    part?"
At times they are before us, at times we gallop past,
Leaving small townships on our way we near the hills at
    last.
Those mountains stand before us ; oh ! what a glorious
    sight,
Could any gaze upon them but with feelings of delight?
Some are quite black and woody, some almost bare
    between,
With here and there some sunny spot, so beautiful and
    green.
By the roadside here are wagons, the horses out at ease,
We hear the sounds of voices, see the people 'mid the
    trees ;
Now we meet happy couples, some who have strolled
    away—
What induces them to leave the sports it is not mine to
    say.
See that lovely sheet of water, it is the Reservoir,
I've often heard about it, but was never here before ;
Now we enter a narrow cutting—high walls on either side,
With space for nought to pass us as two abreast we ride,
With these prison-walls around us ; above, the vault of
    blue,
A hundred yards the cutting pass'd, how changèd is the
    view !

    A narrow mountain pass we tread,
    One side the rocks hang overhead,
    So to look up we almost dread,

Lest they should lose their hold,
And with a loud and angry crash
Down right upon our pathway dash,
Or be perhaps slowly rolled.
No fence the other side to keep
From falling down the stony steep,
Where at the bottom we espy
The River Torrens running by ;
There children out for a holiday
Have sought its bed as best for play,
Perchance indulging in the wish
To catch some unsuspecting fish,
Or, what is more a child's delight
To dabble in its waters bright
When sure they're safe and out of sight.
Another picnic, I declare,   •
Just see the crowds of people there ;
Here 'bus and wagon, cart and dray,
All made do duty for to-day.
We pass where 'neath the gum-trees' shade
A snow-white dinner cloth is laid ;
However well-filled it has been
But scanty fragments now are seen ;
While empty bottles lying near
Tell some are friends of Bacchus here ;
Some dance, and some at croquet play,
Some on the greensward idly lay.
A little on, the river bends,
And there our path abruptly ends.
Full twelve miles we have come from home,
Our horses, reeking wet with foam
Have never wished to slacken speed,

The willing creatures rest must need.
Our friends from out their saddles bound
Gallantly help us to the ground ;
Beside their own our horse they lead,
Across the stream to rest and feed ;
I cannot think they'll safely tread,
Enormous boulders form the bed.
Their iron hoofs strike on the stones,
They slip ! I fear some broken bones ;
But no, so carefully they lead,
They're over safe—I'm glad indeed.
When tied securely to a fence,
A little journey we commence.
The river here, scarce one doth seem,
So nearly dry, 'tis but a stream ;
From stone to stone, it is not wide,
We step and gain the other side,
Then pass the Weir, its thick stone walls
Contain the water as it falls.
More people—some are fishing here,
Some wander on beyond the Weir.
Hills on each side ; thus in a hollow
A narrow little path we follow,
Where the Scotch thistles growing thick,
Pierce through our boots with cruel prick,
Which causes each now and again
To raise the injured limb in pain.
We halt, some sandwiches to eat,
Where a bank serves us for a seat,
Our friends reclining at our feet.
The ride has made us hungry feel,
We relish much our rustic meal ;

With pure cold water, well supplied,
From the river running close beside.
But what if there are reptiles here !
We talk until we almost fear
Lest some shall their appearance make,
In shape perhaps of hideous snake ;
But since they interrupt us not,
Soon their existence is forgot.
'Mid pleasant fun and merry joke,
Our friends produce cigars to smoke ;
And when refresh'd by aid of flask,
Will they not sing a song we ask ?
Of course they can't remember one ;
But listen ! Harry has begun ;
Of " fifty years ago" he sings,
How very different then were things.
A little further on we tread,
Still keeping near the river's bed,
And find some seats—enough of these—
In shape of stones and fallen trees.
Another portion of a song
·From Harry, short and sweet, not long,
While Tom will only snatches sing,
To which the old hills answer ring.
So full of fun, I never saw
Our friends look happier before ;
And of myself I'll only say
I never more enjoyed a day ;
Seated upon a huge block of stone,
Happy as a queen upon her throne :
Such rapture here my bosom fills,
They bid me speak, these noble hills !

" O charming scene ! O lovely spot !
Once to be seen, never forgot :
I gaze around on either side,
Beholding these, Australia's pride ;
Such beauty never would grow tame,
At morn, at eve, 'twould charm the same ;
At morn when all lay hushed and still,
To paint the sun light up yon hill,
Would baffle truest artist's skill ;
When nature seemed to wake and shout,
Then were it mine to wander out
Alone, or with some valued friend
Our purest aspirations blend,
Together on such glories look,
Together study nature's book.
Rich theme for thought thou dost afford:
Admiring thee, man seeks thy God,
And when, at witching hour of eve,
The world its din and bustle leave
The city —pride and work of man—
Here the Almighty's work to scan
Would quell each selfish coarse desire,
And bid our nature to aspire.
Man's narrow mind would here expand,
Beholding all so good, so grand.
Methinks, as I gaze on thee now,
Would that my friends were firm as thou —
That 'mid life's changes they could be
As true and as unchanged as thee."

So soon the afternoon has passed,
The sun does lengthened shadows cast,

On all so bright a shade is thrown,
It bids us be returning home.
Adieu ! fair scene ; oh ! may it be
Mine soon again to visit thee ;
Long wilt thou in my memory dwell,
Like pleasant dream, but fare-thee-well.

The wind has risen from a breeze ;
At times like hurricane so high
With a wild sound it rushes by,
Then softens to a gentle sigh
Among the sheaoak trees.
The tinkling of a bell we hear,
On the hilltop some sheep appear ;
The sheep-boy and his trusty guide
Are climbing up the steep hillside,
The wanderers to their fold to take ;
All warns us it is getting late.
We turn our steps, the river cross,
And soon again have sprung to horse ;
Here we have been the last to stay,
All other folks are gone away,
And behind scarce is seen a trace
To mark where was their resting place.
The laugh and shouts that met our ear,
Have died away—we nothing hear,
Save the little river down below,
Its murmuring waters running slow.
Now, as we through the gullies ride,
But silence reigns on either side,
Our horses' hoofs the echoes waken,
No pic-nic have we yet o'ertaken ;

'Tis pleasant now, at times our way
Bright with the sun's declining ray,
Then dull again, as on we ride,
O'ershadowed by the dark hillside.

We are leaving the hills, but gaze with delight
On what lies before us—magnificent sight !
Below, as mere specks, the small villages lay,
A stillness pervades all at closing of day ;
Like huge fiery ball far off in the west,
Old Sol, in his glory, is sinking to rest ;
Beneath him the sea so bright and so clear,
Far away, yet we truly can fancy it's near,
I gaze on its waters until almost sure
I can see the waves sport—hear them break on the
    shore.
Our horses so free, we give them the rein,
Away we are galloping over the plain ;
Not weary myself, I think what a pity,
So lovely an eve, to be nearing the city ;
About eight o'clock we pass the town through,
Meeting now and again with a picnic or two ;
The ride home so pleasant, when just upon eight
As merry as ever we entered our gate.
In conclusion, I'll add, my best I have tried
To pen an account of " Our Holiday Ride."

SABBATH AT SEA.

[IN THE TROPICS.]

Within the tropics, lulled the breeze which stirred
Our sails, the water's splash no longer heard ;
Above the tall masts mocking rise,
In the dull hue of tropic skies,
The clouds hang stationary over head,
Old ocean seems to slumber in his bed ;
No ripple on his glassy surface seen,
Where bright blue crested waves have been ;
So calmly peaceful, scarce a breath of air,
O how enjoyable this hour of prayer,
And while we pray we know that many more
Are kneeling too in prayer upon the shore ;
Remembering we commit us to the care
Of Him whose arm is outstretched everywhere ;
Who guards the unfledged sparrow in its nest,
And gives to wandering seabird place of rest ;
Teaches yon little nautilus so frail
Upon the wave its tiny bark to sail.
We raise our eyes around, above,
Where all is teaching " God is love ;"
Thousands of miles behind us lay,
Where He has marked our vessel's way ;
Father, what goodness Thou hast shown
In guiding us through paths unknown :
So guide us when this voyage o'er,
We part, perchance, to meet no more ;
And keep us, Lord, as near to Thee
As when in peril on the sea.

EVENING PRAYER AT SEA.

[A FELLOW PASSENGER BEING MUCH WORSE, WHO
DIED THE DAY AFTER REACHING HOME OF
COMSUMPTION.

Holy Father, hear O hear us
From Thy throne in yonder skies,
Thou we know art ever near us,
Seeing him who suffering lies.

For ourselves, Lord, we ask nothing,
Thou hast graciously supplied
Every earthly blessing to us,
Health Thou hast not us denied.

Thus with thankful hearts we seek Thee,
Lend, O Lord, attentive ear,
While we pray for our sick brother,
On his couch reclining near.

Lord, we do not dare to question,
Ask not the appointed time ;
For we trust Thou wilt receive him,
In those blessèd arms of Thine.

But we see how fast he's sinking,
And with pitying hearts implore ;
While from death there is no shrinking,
Spare him till he reach the shore.

Strengthen him, dear Lord, we pray Thee,
  That, supported by Thy hand,
He may join his own—his kindred—
  In his distant fatherland.

Guard our vessel, guide her safely
  Far across the ocean wide ;
May we all, with our sick brother,
  Safely reach the other side.

Safe, at last, reach that blest haven
  Where no storms of earthly strife,
Where no sickness, sin, or sorrow
  Mar the bliss of endless life.

PARTINGS.

Partings, frequent partings,
   In this world of ours ;
They come amid our pleasures,
   Like thorns among fair flowers.

Partings, bitter partings,
   Hearts with fond hearts blend ;
Then the happy dream is over,
   Friend is far from friend.

Painful separations,
   Oceans vast divide ;
Still sweet messages of love
   Span the waters wide.

Who has not known partings,
   Keener sorrow felt,
Watched beside some sick one,
   By the dying knelt ?

Felt the slender fingers
   Grow chilly to the touch ;
Seen death's dew gather on pale brow
   Of one we lovèd much?

Oh ! the lonely feeling,
   When the dead we mourn,
Once they stood beside us,
   Now we know they're gone.

Life is made up of partings
   While here below we dwell ;
But in that happy world above,
   No partings—no farewell.

VANISHED HOPES.

Hopes like earth's fair flowers we cherish,
  Cherish so tenderly till they die !
In our hearts' inmost recesses,
  Then the withered fragments lie ;
Oftentimes a faded blossom,
  Precious made by sorrow's tear,
Treasured for the sake of lost one,
  So are lost hopes, doubly dear !

Ah ! the golden dreams which vanished
  Just when near to be fulfilled,
And the many wild heart cravings,
  Longings which have all been stilled.
Merciful God so oft denies us,
  Much we strive hard to obtain,
In the cherished hope and the golden dream
  Were hidden, perhaps, some bitter pain.

DEDICATION OF AN INFANT.

Precious infant, now we see thee,
  Pure and spotless, undefiled,
And pray God to bless and keep thee
  So through life, sweet darling child.

Lord, be with her from this hour,
  Though we know she cannot be
In the world without some trials,
  From its evils keep her free.

During years when youth unwary
  Oft inclines to go astray,
Thee, O God, we ask to lead her,
  Show her wisdom's happy way.

In all times, should sore temptation
  Meet her in unguarded hour,
Calm the restless heart's wild longings
  By Thy Spirit's gentle power.

Grant her grace to flee all danger,
  That might mar her future life ;
Keep her in the path of virtue,
  Where is neither sin nor strife.

Shield in childhood's days this sweet one,
   Guard her blushing maidenhood,
Till in future years a woman,
   We behold her pure and good.

Give her grace to know and love Thee,
   Grow as Thou would'st have her grow,
In her inmost heart adore Thee—
   Glorify Thy name below.

All our lives are in Thy keeping,
   Fragile babe, grey-headed sire,
Every heart by nature sinful,
   Let Thy love her soul inspire.

To Thee we present this infant,
   Be her Father evermore ;
Guard and guide her through life's journey,
   Lead her Home when life is o'er.

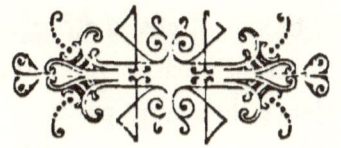

NEVER NURSE A SORROW.

Never nurse a sorrow,
  Or clasp it to thy breast ;
'Twould turn sunshine into sadness
  And banish nightly rest.

If you cherish one small sorrow,
  It will to many turn ;
God is teaching you a lesson,
  Dare you refuse to learn.

This is a life of discipline,
  Perplexity and care ;
Of brooding over trouble,
  O, foolish heart, beware.

If sickness be thy portion,
  Think of painless life above ;
And fix the eye of faith upon
  That home of light and love.

And though it cost a struggle
  Youthful pleasures to forego,
To leave the sunny paths of life
  Where brightest flowerets grow.

Think of many years of health,
  When prosperity was thine ;
When threatened by no tempest
  Thou wert gladden'd by sunshine.

If it be sad separation,
   That bitterest of pain—
Bereavemement—of dearest bonds
   The severing in twain.

Loss of a soul's companion,
   A life linked with thine own ;
One in love, and work, and feeling,
   Death parted, now alone.

O, do not nurse thy sorrow,
   Nor strive to see the end ;
He has taken one too dear to thee,
   To be Himself thy Friend.

Be it blight of disappointment,
   A cruel carking care,
Crushing all fondly-cherished hopes.
   And fostering despair.

O, fear to nurse such sorrow,
   Rather, weak heart, be brave ;
'Twould embitter all thy future,
   Or bring thee to the grave.

O, never nurse a sorrow,
   Never let it to thee cling ;
'Twould sap all happiness from life,
   And prove a deadly thing.

Nor stay to struggle with it.
   It would but fiercer grow :
Up, work, and in the busy world
   Forget you have a foe.

THE WORLD IS WHAT WE MAKE IT.

The world is what we make it, and not what it is made,
Blessings and sunny spots abound for every rank and
    grade ;
'Tis the heart we carry in us forms the world in which we
    live,
And Nature's countless wonders instructive lessons give.

The man who sits with folded hands, the morbidly in-
    clined,
And he of energy and will with a well balanced mind,
Will tell you vastly different tales anent this world of ours:
One desecrates his manhood, one engages all his powers.

One starts a laggard on life's race, and, raising listless eyes,
Will count the clouds if he perchance find any in the skies ;
But no ambition fires his breast nor urges him to try
To excel his fellow creatures who pass frequent briskly by.

If obstacles obstruct his way he fears to further go,
And makes no desperate effort to lay the spectre low,
Sits by the wayside in the shade to wait till it has gone,
Deeming himself the most unfortunate of any creature
    born.

Brooding he waits, his weak heart growing faint and
    fainter till
The spectre grows more terrible the longer he sits still.

Bright flowers that bloom around him his eye no longer
    sees,
Nor his ear doth note the songsters as they warble in the
    trees.

Or if he does, but wonders why the foolish birds do sing
In such a place where nobody is likely crumbs to fling.
Each little bird might lesson teach of lives more wisely
    spent
On building nests, and rearing young, and seeking food
    intent.

When troubles come, when nests are spoiled, not long
    they sit and fret,
But on the wing soon start and sing of better fortune yet.
Why cannot he his burden lift, and with it on his back
With cheerfulness and courage, press on life's beaten
    track.

He tarries yet, there passes by a man at eager pace.
Upon his shoulders ponderous load, yet he with happy
    face ;
In hearty tones his way to cheer sings forth "Excelsior ;"
I will not rest here in the shade, it's brighter on before.

The burden's getting lighter and man must do his work,
The back is for the burden made, 'tis only cowards shirk ;
Better a weary body than diseased or unused brain,
For ease comes sweeter purchased by the sweat of brow
    and pain.

Oh ! this is a happy world, notwithstanding all its strife,
If wisdom guides man's footsteps and religion crowns his
    life.
For trouble gives to character a sweet refining strength,
And lives are measured by deeds wrought, and not by
    length.

Young lives are linked yet closer, love purest pleasures
    give,
When struggling on unitedly for wherewithal to live.
The poor man's babe with rounded limbs a treasure too
    as great
As the infant reared in mansion grand and heir to proud
    estate.

That child how oft in future years a nobler truer man,
For misfortune's sterner discipline when early life began.
Yes, "life is worth the living" if the soul's with wisdom
    stored,
And man's high labours show that he's "the noblest work
    of God."

LITTLE CHILD AT PRAYER.

Know'st thou a picture in this world more fair
To gaze upon than little child at prayer ;
Though many years have flown, methinks I feel
A little form where oft it used to kneel
Upon my lap, while the soft, clear moonlight
Streamed through the casement on her robe of white ;
Around her shoulders fell bright locks of gold,
Methought no angel fairer to behold.
One long look at the moon, the starlit skies,
Then little hands were folded, closed bright eyes,
Rosy lips parted sweetly lisped the prayer
Floating like heavenly music on the air ;
'Twas finished —soon as I had ceased to speak
A loving kiss was pressed upon my cheek,
With pretty, pleading tone and winning smile,
" Auntie, do let me stay a little while,
Tell me about the moon and twinkling star ;
Mamma's in heaven ; is heaven very far ?"
My fingers played with thy soft, silky hair
The while I spoke of heaven ; thy mother there.
Too young to feel thy loss, thou did'st not even cry
When lifted on her bed she prayed her last "good-bye."
Too young to know that parting with her who gave thee
    birth
Was parting with a blessing thou could'st not find on
    earth.

Sweet innocent ! in future years amid life's sin and care
May'st thou, as when a simple child, oft kneel to Him
    in prayer ;
In sorrow, in perplexity, whatever may betide,
Ever while journeying through life strong in His faith
    abide,
So that at last when life is o'er, where all is bright and
    fair,
Among the white-robed saints above thou'lt kneel to
    Him in prayer.

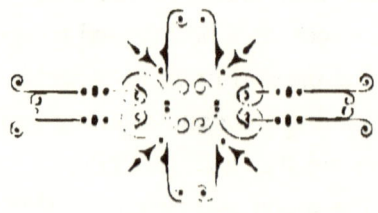

DREAMING.

Methought I was out on the ocean, our vessel
  Was gallantly ploughing the mountainous sea ;
On deck I stood watching the blue-crested billows,
  Dashing the beautiful spray around me.

I descried nought around us as evening drew near,
  Not a vessel nor even a bird hove in sight :
Till I saw in the dark sky a lone star appear,
A beacon to guide us on that stormy night.

Methought in my berth I was sleeping ; awaking,
  The land of my birth had been sighted so near ;
On her shore in the distance I watched the surf breaking,
  And the breeze bore familiar sounds soon to mine ear.

Next, our vessel lay anchored, loved faces I saw,
  And dear voices fondly were greeting ;
I felt my hand grasped, I was hurried ashore,
  O how I had longed for that meeting.

Methought it was Christmas, there hung on the walls
  The holly and mistletoe gay ;
While sounds of high merriment rang through the halls,
  And festivity held happy sway.

Just then I awoke disappointed and sad,
  For, all I remembered so well,
In dreamland I'd wandered so happy and glad,
  But day's-dawn had broken the spell.

THE WRECK OF THE GOTHENBURG.

[HAPPENED FEBRUARY 24, 1875, ON THE GREAT
BARRIER REEF, NOT FAR FROM CAPE BOWLING
GREEN, ON THE COAST OF QUEENSLAND]

The vessel steamed upon her way
At morn— at light of evening grey
A wreck upon the reef she lay.

A tempest swept the sea across,
Driving her from her onward course
Upon the rock with sudden force.

When human souls—her precious freight—
Were thinking not of danger great,
Dreaming not of their awful fate.

Till night fast closing on them there,
The stoutest hearts fill with despair,
And feeblest hands are clasp'd in prayer.

The heavens with black clouds overcast,
Fierce lightning flashing round the mast,
And chilly night-winds howling past.

The dark sea dashing wildly round,
The angry waves with frantic bound
Breaking against with deafening sound.

Two boats lowered from the vessel's side,
Manned by a few, powerless to guide,
Are drifted on the ocean wide.

Tossed to and fro, each crested wave
Baffling every effort to save,
Threatening with a watery grave.

The captain hails them from the deck ;
But further, further from the wreck,
One sinks, one drifts, a tiny speck.

Again by the lightning's flash he saw
The shattered boat moving the water o'er,
Then it broke up on the distant shore.

Cast on a lone isle the four men brave
Who had escaped the yawning grave,
But where the many they could not save

Still the hurricane swept the main,
The deafening thunder pealed forth again
Amid lightning's flash and driving rain.

The awful blackness of sea and sky,
No pitying moon looked from on high
As the cold surges went sweeping by.

The vessel lay still through the fearful blast,
Anxious hearts watching the long night past
For coming of day, till it breaks at last.

She is filling below, they cannot check
The water, the waves wash over the deck :
She slides, and is settling down fast a wreck.

On her deck watching together there,
Men greyheaded with years and care,
Earth's young and beautiful, bravest and fair,

Straining dim eyes to see the shore,
Where are loved ones they shall see no more
Till heaven grant it when life is o'er.

Breathing forth prayers in their sad alarm ;
" O Lord, protect Thy servants from harm.
Speak Peace ! be still ! the troubled sea calm,

" As when of old Thy disciples to save,
When they were afraid, rebuked wind and wave.
Good Lord, deliver us from this grave."

Husband clasped closer his darling wife,
Watching the angry billows' strife,
Feeling they craved for his dear one's life.

Mother, her face white with terror wild,
Pressed to her bosom weak helpless child,
While it, sweet babe, unconsciously smiled ;

Even while safer she thought, it had gone,
Out of those tender arms rude waves had borne,
Leaving not long bereaved parent to mourn.

Gazing out after it into the deep
Wondering whether to tarry or leap,
Swept away, too, with her infant to sleep.

Sisters, dear sisters, so fondly embraced,
Clasping frail arms round each others waist,
Calmly and bravely cruel death faced.

Strong man beside his sick friend stood near,
Whispered encouraging words in his ear,
Bidding him trust One above and not fear.

But the waves little heed whom they divide ;
Snatched is the weak from the stronger one's side,
Floated away on the merciless tide.

Frail tender woman so silently crept
Down where her treasures yet peacefully slept,
Gazed on her helpless ones, trembled and wept.

Kissed the bright rosy lips and knelt beside,
While in soul agony to God she cried :
Drowned, ere the prayer on her pale lips had died.

Lowered now the last boat all that can save ;
Crowded, it soon sinks beneath the wave,
Plunging all in one cold common grave.

A few on the deck—it contained not the whole—
Over them now the huge breakers roll,
Leaving behind not one living soul.

Borne by the mighty billows away,
Struggling to reach, if perchance they may,
The upturned boat as it floating lay.

A few men swim bravely and gain at last
The shipside and make for the standing mast,
Catch at the rigging and cling there fast.

But on the pale, heated cheek falls a tear
From eyes of brave men who never knew fear—
Shed o'er the women and men drowning near.

What are their feelings, alas, none can tell,
As on their ear strikes the funeral knell,
The ocean's roar, and the faint farewell.

To rescue others their brave hearts desire,
E'en though the breakers dash higher and higher.
In their exertions they faint not nor tire ;

But, quickly, ropes in the ocean they cast,
Bidding the struggling ones catch and hold fast,
Thus dragging several up to the mast.

Lashing themselves to the rigging tight,
Fourteen hold on through the stormy night,
Anxiously watching the morrow's light.

'Tis daybreak : the boat floats still on the wave ;
If they but had it, it yet might save ;
Then swam to right her, one young and brave.

So heavy the sea, the breakers so strong,
To lose his life to gain it were wrong ;
He returns—to venture again ere long.

Four times thus bravely he swam out before
His comrades, anxiously watching him, saw
He had gained and succeeded in turning it o'er.

'Tis brought to the vessel ; their great work done.
In her, wet, cold, and exhausted each one :
Brave men, their rescue how nobly they won.

Twenty-two saved.   Men of every rank,
More than a hundred souls there sank
Beneath the wave by that treacherous bank.

No distinction made by devouring wave :
Australias' greatest, her poorest, and brave,
Statesman and sailor sleep in one grave.

Over all rested one funeral pall ;
One coral reef, now the gravestone of all,
Marks where they wait the Redeemer's call.

With the grief-stricken ones truly we weep
Over their dear ones consigned to the deep,
But One above us is able to keep.

CHRISTMAS.

To friend Father Christmas how hearty our greeting,
   Though he comes not with keen blast nor bright holly
      bough ;
Where the sun in blue skies shines hot at the meeting,
   He's as dear as where icicles circle his brow.

He sees in our southern homes much to delight him,
   Merry laugh, bounding step, and the warm pressing
      hand,
Hearts glowing with kindness so much to requite him ;
   But, the blazing log's missing in this sunny land.

Kind faces he sees in the throng, while he listens
   To the song, as he feels he is loved as of yore ;
He hears his name echoed and marks how eyes glisten
   At remembrance of meetings on far distant shore.

What, though there is oftentimes something to sadden—
   The thought of those missing occasion alloy—
The gathering together of households should gladden,
   For nought can obliterate true Christmas joy.

For this is the day when the babe Christ had birth,
  When God gave His greatest of gifts unto men,
And came in a wonderful manner near earth :
  His love now as great towards His children as then.

Christmas, the season for happiest of feeling,
  Wake up the morning with carols of love ;
Doing kindest of deeds, all old differences healing,
  Realizing that peace which Christ brought from above.

To Australia you come when our winter is ended,
  And spring time is passing—at close of the year.
With corn, fruit, and flowers, your coming's attended,
  Old Christmas, we greet you with hearty good cheer.

IN THE COUNTRY.

O 'tis charming to stay in the country awhile,
When nature seems welcoming us with a smile,
To walk where o'er green grass so soft to the tread,
While noble gum branches stretch thick overhead.

To wake in the morn and hear all around
The magpie's rich notes, so flutelike in sound ;
Throw open the casement and feel the soft breeze,
And list to its murmuring song in the trees.

To watch golden sunbeams, as dancing they fall
Through the leaves of the creeper which shadows the wall ;
To stroll and to gather bright wild flowers that grow,
And start the gay butterflies off to and fro.

SLEEPING.

Sleeping—poor tired one—all suffering past,
The sleep thou'st often prayed for come at last :
Thy pain-marred body with its cross laid down ;
Thy spirit gone to wear the victor's crown.
Ah ! happy soul, far happier where thou'rt gone,
I could not wish thee from that blessèd bourne ;
But tarry here, and, wrestling with earth's sin,
Wilt sigh for rest thou now hast entered in.
Released from earthly trouble, freed from pain,
If great our loss, far greater is thy gain.
With aching hearts we grieved to see thee stand
Long on the borders of that spirit land :
Growing far dearer to us day by day,
That slow disease was sapping life away,
But, with sweet patience, striving to fulfil
Upon a sickbed all thy Father's will ;
Endeavouring to drain the bitter cup—
Resignedly, to give thy loved ones up.
Midst greatest suffering, yet relief from pain
Brought the sweet, patient, cheerful smile again ;
Chastened, because so loved of God. 'Tis o'er,
Thou'lt never feel the touch of sorrow more.
Thrice happy soul, why shed another tear ?
Brighter thy crown for all thy suffering here :
Sleeping—poor tired one, both peace and rest
Are thine, reposing on thy Saviour's breast.
He took thee hence, where nought can work thee harm ;
Thy poor frail bark is moored in waters calm ;
The thought supports me now amid my tears,
We're parted only for a few short years.

THE WANDERER'S FAREWELL.

He watches from the vessel's deck
The shore recede, till a mere speck ;
Then in the distance fades away
Port Adelaide, and Holdfast Bay ;
And, clinging to the vessel's side,
Gives way to grief he cannot hide.
" Farewell, my native land, to thee ;
My straining eyes no longer see
Thy shore, once dearest spot on earth,
My childhood's home, land of my birth,
Where earliest years were passed away
In happy innocence at play.
Alas ! where I a boy began
To ape the follies of a man.
Farewell, mine eyes will nevermore
Behold thee, fair Australia's shore ;
Never again thy glorious sun
Shall I see rise, more glorious none ;
Thy gentle moon's bewitching light,
No other moons can shine so bright ;
Behold no more thy fertile plain
Covered with harvest's richest grain ;
Thy stately gums and climbing vine
Once I could claim—no longer mine.
I've looked my last upon thy hills,
Whose grandeur every bosom fills ;

THE WANDERER'S FAREWELL.

My wandering feet no more will stand
Upon thy soil, my native land.
For thee and thine I would not grieve,
But there my mother's dust I leave.
They who were dear no longer are.
My sinful ways put friends afar :
Friendless, and homeless now I roam.
Farewell, my native land, my home.

TO MY PEN.

From time to time, as I sit down to write—
So little leisure, yet such sweet delight
To hold thee, pen, and let thee trace
The thoughts that through my brain give chase.
O were a poet's powers mine,
It were not such insipid rhyme.
Yet, still, thou art my truest friend ;
With thee I happiest moments spend.
For when my heart is light and free
I sit and share its joy with thee ;
And when 'tis sad and full of pain,
With heavy heart and weary brain,
I seek for comfort not in vain.
There's not a shadow in life's sky
But turns to sunshine, with thee nigh.

W. K. Thomas & Co., Printers, Adelaide.

www.ingramcontent.com/pod-product-compliance
Lightning Source LLC
Chambersburg PA
CBHW032011010726
47493CB00007B/2346